Virgil Anson Lewis

Life and Times of Anne Bailey

The pioneer heroine of the Great Kanawha Valley

Virgil Anson Lewis

Life and Times of Anne Bailey
The pioneer heroine of the Great Kanawha Valley

ISBN/EAN: 9783337194406

Printed in Europe, USA, Canada, Australia, Japan

Cover: Foto ©Raphael Reischuk / pixelio.de

More available books at **www.hansebooks.com**

LIFE AND TIMES

—OF—

ANNE BAILEY,

THE PIONEER HEROINE

—OF THE—

GREAT KANAWHA VALLEY,

—BY—

VIRGIL A. LEWIS,

SECRETARY

WEST VIRGINIA HISTORICAL AND ANTIQUARIAN SOCIETY.

Corresponding Member of the Virginia Historical Society; Member
Pennsylvania Historical Society; Corresponding Member of the
Western Reserve Historical Society of Cleveland; and Au-
thor of the "History of West Virginia."

———

'Out of monuments, names, wordes, proverbs, traditions, priva'e records, frag-
ments of stories, passages of bookes and the like, we doe save and
recover somewhat from the deluge of time."—*Bacon.*

———

CHARLESTON, W. VA.:
THE BUTLER PRINTING COMPANY.
MDCCCXCI.

PREFACE.

Is it possible at this late date to save from oblivion the Pioneer History of West Virginia? What shall the answer to this question be? That much of that history is now lost—gone with those who were the principal actors in the drama—is certain, but that very much yet remains and with proper effort, may be preserved from the ruthless hand of oblivion, is equally certain.

Our history is not so nearly lost as we are by some led to believe, and if this be true, then what is the chief source from which it can be preserved? I answer, from persons yet alive. In every county in the state there are many persons now living at the age of from sixty to eighty years old who were themselves acquainted with the actors in the border scenes when they were of like age. This carries us backward an hundred and twenty years, to the year 1770, so that for one hundred years at least, we may have a

narrative of events, coming to us from credita-
ble witnesses yet living, who learned the *facts*
to which they testify, from those who were themselves the actors in and witnesses of the scenes
of which they have transmitted oral accounts.
This is competent testimony, such as would be
received in evidence in any court in the state.

Will our history be preserved? Judging from
the present activity on all hands, and the increasing inquiry relative to the local and family
history of our people now heard on every hand,
the answer to this question must be an affirma-
tive one. To-day in many counties of the state,
local historians are busy collecting the traditions and reminiscences of their localities; the
press of the state is devoting attention to this
and kindred subjects, and state officials are for
the first time collecting and putting in durable
form the reports and public documents of the several departments, while books are rapidly multi-
plying in the state. Foremost in the task of collecting and preserving, stands the West Virginia
Historical and Antiquarian Society, an organization which is bending every energy to the work
before it and with the forces now employed we pre-
dict that soon all of the past now possible to save

from the ruthless hand of time, will be gathered in its archives. But the work must be prosecuted rapidly. Time is passing hastily by and laying its blighting hand upon material things and with such destroying effects, that there remains not a year for suspended action. "Now or never." must bs the watch-word of our people if they would preserve their own history and transmit it to those who are to come after them.

The following pages compose a mite of the work to be accomplished and no apology is therefore deemed necessary for its appearance.

V. A. L.

Charleston, W. Va.

✦ANNE BAILEY,✦

THE PIONEER HEROINE OF THE GREAT KANAWHA VALLEY.

—✦✦✦—

CHAPTER I.

THE HERO WOMEN OF THE WEST.

The women who accompanied their husbands, brothers and sons in the march of civilization and the conquest of the wilderness were Spartans in all that the term implies. The embodiment of all that ennobles womankind, they possessed in a wonderful degree, a complete union of strength, courage, love, devotion, meekness and shrewdness which fitted them for the severe and often terrible ordeals through which they had to pass. Not only did they share the hardships and privations of frontier life, but they were familiar with war's dread alarm. From infancy to old age, from the

cradle to the grave, their ears were saluted with
the story of savage war fare, the reprisal, the
ambuscade, the midnight burning, the stake, the
scalping knife and the rencounters of rifle and
tomahawk, were all familiar to them. But disre-
garding danger, toil and suffering and alone devoted to the safety of those composing their little
households gathered in the cabin homes of the
western border, these mothers and daughters
nerved their arms and steeled their hearts to the
severe duties that surrounded them. It was the
Heroic Age of America and these the hero
mothers of the Western Border and of the Revolution.

Other ages and other lands, have produced
women whose names are famous on the historic
page. Indeed history is replete with examples
of female heroism. Israel had her Deborah;
Spain delights to dwell upon the memory of
Isabella; while France glories in the names of her
Joan of Arc and Lavellette. But two of these
women unsexed themselves in the excitement of
battle, one ingloriously stained her hands in human blood, and the other had nothing to lose by
her successful efforts.

But the western heroines of our own land,

without the *eclat* of female warriors, displayed more true courage throughout the long and stormy days of the Indian wars, and exhibited more of the true spirit of heroism, than any examples in ancient times or in modern history beyond our own land. The Greek matron who urged her son to the conflict charging him to return from the war with his shield, or see her face no more, displayed no higher degree of true courage, than did these Hero Women of the West. One of these has left her name indellibly impressed upon the pages of the history of the Great Kanawha Valley and the story of her life and adventures still lives in the traditions of the people. Several incidents relating to her, have been published, but no western chronicler has attempted to collect in connected narrative the story of ANNE BAILEY, the Pioneer Heroine of the Valley. In an attempt to do this, these pages have been written.

For generations the traditional history of Anne Bailey has been transmitted from father to son and from mother to daughter, and to-day the traveler can scarcely stop at the home of an old family in the Great Kanawha Valley at which he could not hear some adventure recounted or anecdote related illustrative of the character of this remarkable woman.

But little relating to her has been written, and the major portion of that has been done since her death, and by persons who never saw her; hence, at this late day, we must rely almost entirely upon tradition for what may now be learned of her whose name for a century has been a household word in the valley of the Great Kanawha. But tradition, when accepted by common consent; when divested of everything of a mythical character, and when stripped of the fabulous, the imaginary and the fanciful, then, to the student as well as the writer of history, it becomes competent evidence and as such. has been accepted in all ages of the world's history, as witness the following:

"Stand fast, hold the *traditions* which ye have been taught." 2 Thess. ii. 15.

"Will you mock at an ancient *tradition* begun upon an honorable respect?"—*Shakespeare.*

"Naught but *tradition* remains of the beautiful village of Grand Pre.'—*Longfellow.*

What is tradition? It may be defined as the unwritten delivery of information concerning practices, customs and events transmitted from father to son; from ancestors to descendants, or from one generation to another, and in this sense, it is one of the pillars of written history, and ceases to be tradition and becomes history when it *is* written.

In the following pages everything not consistent with truth has been eliminated and the accuracy of the work rests upon what has been written in the past, relative to the subject, upon records and upon the testimony of witnesses yet living who saw and conversed with Anne Bailey. Among these are Colonel Charles B. Waggener, of Point Pleasant, now in his eighty-fourth year; Mrs. Mary McCulloch, of Mason county, now eighty-one years of age; Mrs. Mary Irions, and Mrs. Phebe Willey, both of Gallia caunty, Ohio, the former in her eighty-fourth year and the latter seventy-four years of age and both grand-daughters of Anne Bailey; Mr. John Slack, Sr., of Charleston, now eighty-two years of age; and Mr. John H. Goshorn, also of Charleston, now in the seventy-eighth year of his age.

CHAPTER II.

That Anne Bailey, whose maiden name was Hennis, was born in England, and that the city of Liverpool was the place of her nativity, is established by an unbroken chain of testimony. She ever prided herself upon being born in England's western metropolis. But of the exact date of her birth, she was not herself certain, and it is safe to say that nothing connected with her history has been the subject of greater exageration than this, and for nearly three-quarters of a century, it has been the current belief and so stated by those who have written of her, that at the time of her death, she was a centenarian, and by some that she died in the one hundred and twenty-fifth year of her age.

Singular it is indeed that such an idea should have obtained when it was *almost* contrary to natural laws, when directly opposed to her own declaration, and when a little investigation would have set the matter right. Let us see what can be learned respecting the date:

Her father was a soldier in the wars with Queen Anne and served on the continent under the duke of Marlborough, where with his regiment, he participated in the desperate battle of Blenheim. Returning to his home and family, he bestowed upon his infant daughter—the child of his old age—the name of *Anne* in honor of his beloved sovereign, whose banner he had so bravely defended in foreign lands.

In the year 1747, the mother, accompanied by the Queen's namesake, went from Liverpool to London to visit her brother, and there for the first time, and probably the last, the little daughter, as she well remembered, witnessed in her wonder and astonishment, the splendors of the British capital.

It was while sojourning in London that an event occurred, which made such a lasting impression upon the child, and the scene then witnessed, wrought so much upon her mind, that all the years of her after life, could not efface it and she talked of it until the time of her death, ever asserting that she was then *five* years of age.

This event was the public execution of Lord

Lovat, upon a charge of treason, and now if we can fix the date of that execution, from which she reckoned time, we can then readily arrive at the *date of her birth.* All English authorities agree as to the time.

Simon Frazer Lovat, was born about the year 1676, and was the second son of Thomas, afterwards the twelfth Lord Lovat. He took his degrees at King's College, Aberdeen, where he gained a good knowledge of the Latin classics.

One of his first acts after leaving school, was to organize a body of three hundred men, ostensibly, to be a part of a regiment in the service of William and Mary and in which he was to hold a commission, but his real purpose, as he afterwards avowed, was to have at his command, a body of trained men, whom he could at any time carry over to the interest of James.

His next act was to bring about a forced marriage with the widow of his elder brother by which he secured the title and estates of the deceased. But the family of Lady Lovat, began a prosecution against him and he fled to the Highlands, and later sought refuge in France, where, by various intrigues, he soon gained favor at the court of Versailles.

From there he directed a secret military organization in the north of Scotland, which arose in the interest of the Pretender in the rebellion of 1745. He then returned to Scotland and after the battle of Colloden fled to the Highlands, where, from the summit of a lofty eminence, he witnessed the burning of his own proud castle of Dounie, laid in ashes by the royal army.

A fugitive, he wandered from place to place, until arrested on a little island in Loch Moras, near the west coast of Scotland. Thence he was taken to London, where, after a trial lasting five days, he was sentenced to death and *was executed on the 9th day of April, 1747,* as Anne Bailey always asserted, when *she was five years of age.*

It certainly exhibits a great lack of investigation on the part of those who have written of her, for without exception, they all assert that she was born about the year 1700, and yet they declare that, according to her own statement, she was five years of age when Lord Lovat was executed. Now, the *fact* is, as she stated, that she was five years of age in 1747, and chat she was born in 1742.

William P. Buell, in a biographical sketch of

Anne Bailey, published in the *Magazine of Western History*, for April, 1885, says: "Anne Bailey was born in Liverpool, England, in the year 1700, and was named in honor of Queen Anne, and was present with her parents at her coronation in 1705." This is evidently incorrect, for Anne *was not crowned in 1705*, as stated, but in 1702. Again he says: "At the age of thirty, she married a man named John Trotter." Here he is wrong again; first, in that her husband's name was not *John* but Richard. Now, that we may see how inaccurate such statements are—and the author quoted has followed all of his predecessors—let us admit as true the statement that she married at the age of thirty. Now, if she was born in the year 1700, as asserted, then she was married in 1730. Then her only son was born *thirty-seven* years after her marriage when she was *sixty-seven* years of age, for it is a matter of record that he was born in the year 1767. Then again, accepting the statement that she was born in 1700, she was then seventy-four years of age when left a widow, lived in a state of widowhood eleven years, married John Bailey at the age of *eighty-five* and made her famous ride from Fort Clendennin to Lewisburg, a distance of one hundred miles, continuing night and day, when she was *ninety-one* years old. Is the student of history asked to believe that which is contrary to nature and to the facts of history? No, it cannot be so. Then let Anne Bailey's testimony stand as authority; and when she says she was *five* years of age when Lord Lovat was executed, let it be recorded that she was born in Liverpool, England, in 1742.

CHAPTER III.

ANNE BAILEY'S MARRIAGE AND RESIDENCE IN THE COLONY OF VIRGINIA.

How or when Anne Baily came to Virginia, is not certainly known, but notwithstanding this, various statements have been made, each asserted to be true. Mr. Buell, before cited, says that: "When a school girl at the age of nineteen, she was kidnapped with her books while on her way to school, brought to America and landed in Virginia, on James River, where she was sold to defray the expense of her passage."

Certainly, this is not a reasonable statement, for it is not at all probable that those who kidnapped her, and brought her across the Atlantic would then have permitted her to be sold into the bondage of others to defray her ship's fare. No authority is given for the statement, presumably, for the reason that there is none.

Mr. Averill, following others, says that: "She

wedded Richard Trotter, with whom she sought a home in the province of Virginia. Because of their extreme poverty, both were 'sold out,' as was then the custom, to defray the expense of their passage. They were bought by a gentleman of the name of Bell, residing in Augusta county, Virginia, where, after their term of service expired they became settlers."

How inconsistent is this. The date given is 1730, which was undoubtedly about *twelve* years before Anne Bailey was born. Again, "they were bought by a gentleman of the name of Bell residing in Augusta county." This can not be true, for every student of Virginia history knows that neither "a gentleman of the name of Bell, nor any other *white man* had found a home in Augusta county at that time. John Lewis was the first settler in Augusta and he reared his cabin home near Staunton, in 1732. This was two years after they declare Anne Bailey, who with her husband, who, they tell us was a brave English soldier, came to serve out a term of bondage in Augusta. How absurd that a brave English soldier should be *sold out* to defray his passage to an English colony.

Now let us see what are the traditions long

popular in Virginia. Anne Bailey spent her childhood days in Liverpool, attended the school in which she learned to read and write, and when she had grown to an adult age, her parents died leaving her with small means, but alone in a great city. Then scarcely knowing what to do, she bethought herself friends, (some say relatives) the Bells in their distant home to which they had gone beyond the sea. Heroine that she was, she determined to follow them, and went on ship-board. The sails were unfurled and the ship stood out on the Irish sea; then the coast line of her native land disappeared from view and later, the blue hills of Ireland faded away in the distance, and thoughts came to her of that far-away strange land to which she was going and in which she was to leave a name to be re-membered, honored and revered long years after she had passed from among the living. In time the capes of Virginia stood out to view, and the ship passed up the James. Then the journey into the wilderness began; the Blue Ridge was passed and the future heroine of the Valley of the Kanawha, in 1761, when in her nineteenth year, found a home and a welcome with the Bells near where Staunton now stands.

Soon after her arrival in Augusta, she became acquainted with Richard Trotter, a brave frontiersman, who was then and had been engaged in defending the border settlements from the incursions of the savages who were then carrying death and destruction into the beautiful Valley of the Shenandoah, even to the base of the Blue Ridge. Amid wild solitudes he had grown to manhood, and nature had made him a nobleman; his manners were rough, like the scenes around him, his mind strong, and his disposition frank and fearless. From his earliest childhood he was saluted with the story of savage warfare, and the recital aroused within him a spirit of adventure and daring and he longed to engage in struggles fierce and wild.

The opportunity soon came. In the spring of 1755, General Edward Braddock arrived at Alexandria, Virginia, with an army composed of the 44th and 48th Royal Infantry Regiments, destined for American service. This force proceeded up the Potomac and at Fort Cumberland —now Cumberland City, Maryland—was joined by a regiment of Virginia Provincials, in the ranks of which were many Valley men, one of them being Richard Trotter, then a mere youth.

The march into the wilderness began. Slowly the splendid pageant moved on, the long lines of scarlet uniforms contrasting strangely with the verdure of the forest, while strains of martial music filled the air—sounds so strange beneath the dark shades of the American forest.

It was the evening of the 8th of July, 1755, when the English columns, for the second time reached the Monongahela at a point—now Braddock's Field—ten miles distant from Fort Duquesne. On the next day a crossing was effected, and once across the stream, the order to advance was given, but the columns were scarcely in motion when Gordon, one of the English engineers, saw the French and Indians bounding through the forest. At once a deadly fire was poured in upon the English, who returned it with little effect. Braddock formed the regulars into squares, as if he had been maneuvering on the fields of Europe, and thus the men were shot down in heaps. Of the twelve hundred who crossed the Monongahela, sixty-seven officers and seven hundred and fourteen privates were either killed or wounded. Braddock was among the fallen, and of all his aids, Washington alone was left. Many Virginians were among the dead, but a

sufficient number were left—among them Richard
Trotter—to form a line and cover the retreat of the
shattered army back to Fort Cumberland, whence
the Virginians returned to their homes, Richard
Trotter going to his, which was near Staunton,
where representatives of the family now reside.

Years went by and there came from over-
sea a maid with fair complexion, hazel eyes, a
perfectly developed form, a sweet disposition, a
mind strong and vigorous, softened by the rudi-
ments of an education, obtained in the schools of
Liverpool. It was Anne Hennis. Richard Trotter
became enamored of her charms. But "none but
the brave deserve the fair;" and none but the
brave could win the heart of Anne Hennis, for,
through her veins coursed the blood of a father
who had served his country long and well, who
had marched under the banner of Queen Anne,
to many bloody and chaotic fields, and no coward
could win the affections of his daughter, even
though she was a stranger on the frontier wilds of
Virginia. But Richard Trotter had long been
engaged in the wars of civilization against bar-
barism, and in him she beheld a soldier, a hero.
This was enough. He had defended the homes
of others, he would defend his own. There was

a pioneer wedding, and Richard Trotter and Anne Hennis, in the year 1765, were made husband and wife.

CHAPTER IV.

A little cabin was reared and to it Richard Trotter took his happy bride. That home was like all others on the Virginia frontier at that day. A clearing of a few acres was made by cutting away the primeval forest which overshadowed the land, the rude cabin was erected, and then the family moved and though, the luxuries of later days were unknown, it became the abode of happiness and contentment, while on all hands was naught but the voiceless wilderness.

Richard Trotter belonged to a class of men of whom it was said: "They are statesmen to-day, farmers to-morrow, and soldiers always." Exposed to a common danger, and sharing alike the toils and privations of the wilderness, they became a distinct class known throughout the Colony as the backwoodsmen of Augusta. They

were clad in the border suit of home-spun, made
by the hands of wives, mothers and daughters.
Heavy buckskin moccasins and leggins were
usually worn, with a hunting shirt and a cap made
of beaver or otter skin; the long rifle was carried
upon the shoulder; the hatchet was swung in the
belt, while the hunting knife was lodged in a
sheath fastened to the strap of the shot-pouch.
Thus equipped, it is difficult to conceive of a
more formidable personage than were these backwoodsmen in full dress, especially when reflect-
ing upon the precision with which they dealt the
missiles of death and their wonderful power to en-
dure the fatigue and hardships, incident to a hunt-
er's life.   Once upon the route thus prepared,
they ranged in summer the valleys beneath the
misty forest, or in winter, scaled the summits of
the bleak and leafless Alleghenies, and, often after
weeks of absence, these backwoodsmen of Augusta, returned to their homes to which even
Washington, in after years expected to be com-
pelled to fly, there, to defend the last faint spark
of liberty.

Beyond the general experience of border life,
we know nothing of the home life of Richard
Trotter and his devoted wife.   In the year 1767,

two years after their marriage, the bond of union which bound them together was doubly cemented by the birth of a son, who was christened William, and who was to be the chief staff of support to the mother in her declining years.

The storm of savage warfare continued to rage along the western border, but its scenes of blood did not deter these hardy frontiersmen from pushing into the wilderness. Pressing over the mountains, a few of the most adventurous established their homes on Muddy Creek, in the Greenbrier country, but short was the sojourn for this germ of civilization planted in the wilderness, perished by the hands of barbarian fury.

Time hastened on and brought the year 1774, and with it the close of the halcyon decade of the eighteenth century. The period of Dunmore's War was ushered in. The vast savage aggregation west of the Ohio, was pressing down upon the frontier of civilization. Virginia made ready for war and the din of preparation resounded along her borders. Lord Dunmore left the gubernatorial mansion at Williamsburg and hastening over the Blue Ridge, assisted in mustering an army. Staunton became a rendesvous, and here hundreds of the backwoodsmen of Augusta

entered the Colonial army. Among those who
plead for volunteers, there was one female voice.
It was the wife of Richard Trotter, encouraging
the men to strike and break the savage power
and thus save the mothers and children of Augusta from the tomahawk and scalping-knife of
the savage.

On a bright September morning long lines of
sturdy men filed away into the wilderness, and
that night, there were many lonely homes throughout Augusta, one of them being the Trotter
homestead, for the father was gone on the fated
march and the shadows of evening gathered
thick around the little cabin in which, alone were
the heroic mother and little son.

The army augmented to eleven hundred men,
left Camp Union—now Lewisburg—and began
the toilsome march of one hundred and sixty
miles to the Ohio. There was not even a track
through the rugged mountains, but the gallant
army moved rapidly through the home of the
wolf, the bear and the panther, and beneath the
autumnal shades of the forest in which the golden
hue of the linden and the maple blended with the
crimson of the sumac, and sombre green of the
laurel and hemlock, and at last left the rocky

mountain tops behind and descended to where the Kanawha and the Elk united, widens into fertile bottoms.

The Elk was passed, the march continued and on the 1st day of October, 1774, the army reached the mouth of the Kanawha, where, on the 10th of the same month, it waged the most fiercely contested battle ever fought with the Indians in Virginia if not on the continent. Indeed, in many aspects, it has no parallel in the annals of forest warfare. That evening as the sun sank behind the low hills of the western wilderness, one hundred and forty wounded Virginians were borne by more fortunate companions into the encampment, while the dead lay scattered over the bloody field. Among the latter was Richard Trotter who, like those who had fallen beside him, had yielded up his life in defence of pioneer homes and in an effort to plant civilization in the Ohio Valley. Such was the scene that October evening at Point Pleasant:

"Where all day long the sound of battle rolled;
Where all day long, the fearful and the bold
Behind their slender bulwarks, stern and pale,
Stood face to face beneath the leaden hail;
Stood face to face, the white man and the red,
Their cause the same, the same their gory bed."

But how different was the scene far away amid the hills of Augusta ! That night as the survivors sat amid the dead and dying at Point Pleasant,

"They thought of dear ones far across the hills,
Of West Augusta homes, where warm and bright
The fire-light gleamed on household gods at night,
And dawn awoke each weary, weary day,
When bright eyes waiting, watched the western way,
For forms those eyes might never, never greet ;
For forms then stark in death,—where two great rivers meet."

Yes, long they watched the western way and at last a message came with the tidings of death, and there was grief and mourning in many Augusta homes. Among them was that of Richard Trotter, where dwelt his widow and orphan son.

CHAPTER V.

A REMARKABLE CAREER OF FEMALE HEROISM —ELEVEN YEARS OF WIDOWHOOD—HER SECOND MARRIAGE.

Wedded at the age of twenty-three, Anne Trotter was a widow at the age of thirty-two, and so remained for eleven years. From the moment she heard of her husband's death, what appeared to be a strange wild dream seemed to possess her, and she resolved to avenge his death. It was far from a visionary dream with her. It was instead the outburst and exhibition of patriotism and heroism combined, as true as was ever evidenced by womankind. No people had ever occupied such a position as those by whom she was surrounded and among whom she lived. The Revolution was now at hand and they were menaced alike by the savage from the wilderness and the Briton from the sea. To the backwoodsmen of the Shenandoah Valley, it was not a war for

liberty but of existence as well, and never was a
rallying cry more needed than there.

But what could Anne Trotter do? She could
not command an army nor bear arms in the wilderness or on the Atlantic sea-board. Then with
a fatherless son, but seven years of age, what was
there for her to do? But she found a field of
duty and tradition tells how well she performed
her part.

Her near neighbor was Mrs. Moses Mann, some
of whose family had fallen victims to savage bar-
barity and to her Anne Trotter explained her
plans of operation. Mrs. Mann, imbued with a
similar spirit, approved all and tendered a home
to the little son, made orphan by a savage bullet
at Point Pleasant, and the mother at once entered upon a career which has no parallel in
Virginia annals.

Clad in the costume of the border she hastened
away to the recruiting stations where she urged
enlistments with all the earnestness which her
zeal and heroism inspired. Her appeals were
first in behalf of the defenceless women and
children of the border, who were constantly exposed to the attacks of the savages, and when
these were not in immediate danger, her voice was

heard, urging men to enlist in the Virginia lines on Continental establishment and strike for freedom in a struggle waged against the Land that gave her birth and in which her parents slept the last long sleep.

Clad in buckskin pants, with petticoat, heavy brogan shoes, a man's coat and hat, a belt about the waist in which was worn the hunting-knife, and with rifle on her shoulder, she went from one recruiting station to another and from one muster to another, making her appeals to all whom she met. The whole border, from the Potomac to the Roanoke, was her field of action, and long ere the Revolution closed, the name of Anne Trotter was famous along the border, and her virtue and heroism were extoled by all who knew her.

At last the Briton was gone. Virginia and her sister colonies were free, but for long years to come, the struggle on the western border was to continue and in this, she now redoubled her energy and afoot or mounted on horse-back, she bore messages between Staunton and the distant frontier forts, among them Fort Fincastle on Jackson's river, Fort Edward on the Warm Spring Mountain, and Fort Loudoun, now Winchester.

In 1778. Fort Savannah—now Lewisburg, in

Greenbrier—was erected and became the most western outpost of civilization, on the southwestern frontier of Virginia, with the single exception of Fort Randolph at Point Pleasant, on the distant banks of the Ohio, and far out in the unbroken wilderness. The former became a favorite objective point for her, and she soon was familiar with every path between Staunton and Lewisburg, along which she bore messages, carried letters, and Staunton awaited her coming with anxiety, for she was a messenger from out the wilderness.

A new field for adventure opened before her. One hundred and sixty miles lay between Lewisburg and Point Pleasant; over the route the army had marched in 1774, and Anne Trotter, no doubt animated by a desire to visit the scene on which crumbled to dust, all that was mortal of her husband, pushed into the wilderness, traversed the lonely defiles of the Allegheny mountains, crossed the Gauley and the Elk, and reached Point Pleasant. Thus she traversed the Valley which was later to be the scene of many of her adventures.

Once more she thought of love and of a fixed habitation. A *soldier* sought her heart and hand.

It was John Bailey and he was one worthy of the prize he sought. Long years he had been in service on the frontier and was at that time engaged with a body of scouts, in defending the Roanoke and Catawba settlements from savage hands. Among his associates were James Bailey, Edward Burgess, John Crockett, James Martin, John Maxwell, Oliver Wynn, and James Witten. They with others, were the rangers of Southwest Virginia and for years they traversed the valleys of the Big Sandy and its tributaries with those of the Holstein and Upper Tennessee. For such a responsible position, only the best men on the border were chosen, for it will readily appear that one faithless spy might have permitted the Indians to pass unobserved along their warpath, when they would have spread carnage and death throughout the settlement before they could have prepared for defense. But it does not appear that even one of these scouts failed to give the alarm and thus save those whose lives they had in their keeping.

These RANGERS always went together and often remained out several weeks upon the scout. Great caution was necessary to prevent the Indians from discovering them; hence their beds were of leaves in the underbrush, or beneath some shelving rock, whence they could overlook the war-path. Scorched by the summer's sun; chilled by the wintry blast, drenched by the driving rain, and pelted by the sleet and hail, these faithful guardians were ever at their posts and with unwearied eye, watched the western way from the heights of the Cumberland and the defiles of the Alleghenies.

What services were performed by these Rangers, led by a Bailey, a Lewis, a McClenachan, a Cunningham, a Preston, a Dickinson, a Clendenin, a Dunlap, or a Moffett, armed and equipped at their own expense, as they marched into the wilderness to punish or disperse hostile bodies of Indians!

There was no engagement ring. There was no embossed, tinted and perfumed wedding invitation cards sent to the friends and relatives of the contracting parties, but there was a wedding at Lewisburg. There was a minister in readiness, whose name will never be lost from the church annals of West Virginia. It was the Rev. John McCue, the first settled Presbyterian minister west of the Alleghenies. He was licensed to preach May 22, 1782, at Timber Ridge Church, in Rockbridge county, and was instructed by Hanover Presbytery to labor in Greenbrier county. Here his pastorate continued more than nine years. Who composed the wedding guests we do not know, but it was a "marriage in high life" and doubtless many of the Pioneers of Greenbrier were there. We may suppose that in the assembly were the scholarly John Stewart, the heroic Andrew Donnally, with representatives from the McClung, Renick, Hamilton families and others. The date was November 3rd, 1785, when the bride was forty-three years of age. The minister pronounced them man and wife and thus Anne *Trotter*, the heroine of the Shenandoah Valley, became Anne *Bailey*, the heroine of the Great Kanawha Valley. The record of the marriage may be seen in Marriage Record No. 1, page 7, in the County Clerk's office at Lewisburg.

CHAPTER VI.

Under Governor Dinwiddie's proclamation, of
1754, Colonel Thomas Bullitt received a patent
for one thousand and thirty acres of land which
he located where Charleston now stands, in 1773.
Soon after he sold it to his brother, Cuthbert Bullitt, of Maryland, who in time transferred the
title to his son, Cuthbert, of Prince William
county.

Prominent on the frontier of Virginia, were
the Clendenins, an old Scotch-Irish family. The
exact date at which they came to Virginia is a
matter of uncertainty, but that they were residing upon "Burden's Grant" as early as 1753, is
shown by the records of Augusta county, where
the family was founded by two brothers, Archibald and Charles. A third brother came to
America but settled at Baltimore, where he be-

came the ancestor of the Clendenins of Maryland. Those in Virginia became daring frontiersmen, satisfied only with a home on the confines of civilization, and this desire to penetrate the wilderness led to the extinction of one branch of the family, Archibald and his family—with the exception of his wife, who escaped from captivity—all perished in the Greenbrier massacre of 1763. It is believed that the other brother, Charles, was married before coming to Virginia. The date at which he removed west of the mountains is not known, but that he with his wife and sons, George, William, Robert, and Alexander, and daughter, Ellen Mary, was residing on Greenbrier river, as early as 1780, is a matter of record.

George, the eldest son, had risen to prominence in both the civil and military affairs of the state, and in 1787, when in Richmond, he met young Bullitt from whom he purchased the lands lying on the Kanawha at the mouth of Elk, and there in 1788, he removed, taking with him his aged father and brothers and sister, the mother being dead. Here these founders of the future capital of West Virginia, reared the walls of a blockhouse, afterwards known on the frontier as Clendenin's Fort, but it should be Fort Lee, for

so it was named in honor of Governor Henry
Lee of Virginia.

Here then was another fort to be garrisoned,
and to it John Bailey went on duty, taking with
him to reside therein, his now famous bride.

Here our heroine entered upon a career un-
surpassed in deeds of daring and adventure, in
the annals of the whole western border. Her
skill with the rifle, the dexterity of equestrian
performance, and her care for the sick and helpless, challenged the admiration of the entire garrison and won for her a name still cherished by
the descendants of these old soldiers.

Often she left the fort and rode away into the
forest and, if the commander wished to send a
message to Fort Randolph at the mouth of the
Kanawha, distant sixty miles away, Anne Bailey
became the messenger, and passing the Elk she
disappeared in the wilderness, and down the Kanawha, over streams, through dense underbrush,
sleeping if need be, with a horse tied to a tree,
and her ears saluted by the howl of the wolf, the
scream of the panther or perchance the warwhoop
of the savage. Back over the same route, she
came bringing the report from the commandant
at Point Pleasant.

These were times that tried men's souls, and only the love of helpless wives and babes moved these frontiersmen to deeds, the performance of which has won for them, names as lasting as heroism itself.

More than a century has passed away, and official records are now our only guide to the condition of affairs then existing in the Valley.

April 15, 1790, Thomas Lewis, at the mouth of the Great Kanawha, wrote Col. George Clendenin, at "Charles Town,"—now Charleston—and said: "It is unnecessary to mention anything respecting the situation other than that they (the people) are collected in bodies and await the moment when the savages make a formidable attack to depopulate the settlements on the Kanawha." Col. Clendenin forwarded the letter to the Virginia war department by private carrier.

The central figure in the military affairs at that time, was Col. George Clendenin. As colonel-commandant of Kanawha county, he was commander-in-chief of the Valley Department. As such, on January 1—New Years's Day—1791, he addressed a letter to Governor Randolph, relative to the western defenses, in which he said: "I beg leave to request the honorable board to consider

the peculiar situation of the county of Kanawha
—then including the entire Valley—and the disposition the Indians have lately exercised against
it and that you and the board will indulge the
county with four scouts, in case the general gov-
ernment may not make such arrangements as the
exposed situation may require. This number, I
am certain, is not sufficient, but they would be
of great service to alarm the inhabitants of the
approach of the enemy, so as to enable them to
collect together to secure themselves from savage
cruelty. I feel myself disposed to make this last
request from the most tender motives of affection
for my own family and the lives of my friends
and neighbors equally exposed."

On the 12th day of December, 1791, Daniel
Boone, the founder of Kentucky, but then residing in the Valley and holding the position of
Lieutenant-Colonel of Kanawha county, wrote
Governor Henry Lee, regarding the military establishment of the county. His letter is charac-
teristic of the man who wrote it :

"For Kanaway County, 68 Privits; Lenard
Cuper, Captain, at Pint plesent, 17 men; John
Morris, Juner, Insine at the Bote yards 17 men.
Two spyes or scutes Will be Nessesry at the

pint to sarch the Banks of the River at the Cross-ing places. More would be Wanting if the(y) could be aloude. Those Spyes Must be Com-poused of the inhabitence who Well Know the Woods and Wators from the pint to belleville, 60 mildes—No inhabitence; also from the pint to Elke, 60 mildes—No inhabitence; from Elke to the Bote yards, 20 mildes, all inhabited."

Here we are officially informed that in the year 1791, there was not a white inhabitant in all the Kanawha Valley, from Point Pleasant to Fort Charleston, while from the same source we learn that at that time the cabin homes of the pioneers dotted the banks of the Kanawha from the last named place to the "Bote yards" by which Boone refers to the mouth of Kelly's Creek.

Amid such trying scenes, lived the first set-tlers of the Valley, and who that looks backward over the lapse of a century, does not fondly cher-ish all that pertains to their memory?

CHAPTER VII.

Let the mind go backward just a hundred
years, to 1791, and view the site on which
Charleston with its busy scenes and cultured
population, now stands.

There are the same plains, valleys and hills;
the same rivers flowed calmly on then as now.
In the forests that overhung the banks, the buds
had bursted and the green leaves betokened the
advance of summer. The beautiful Kanawha,
fresh from its mountain springs flowed on in its
majesty, as yet its waters unstained by the
murky tide of the Ohio. The stately forest on
the broad bottoms was so dense, that it almost
shut out the light of day, while the trunks of the
giant trees were festooned with the ivy and the
honeysuckle, and the boughs entwined with the

grape. On every hand rose the verdant hills, like towers, the work of no human hands, and on their fertile slopes, among the hazel and the alder, flowered the blue-bells and bleeding-hearts.

Amid this scene of inspiring beauty, down close by the brink of the Kanawha, stood Fort Lee. Day unto day the agents of civilization found refuge within its walls. Night came and they repeated the story of struggles fierce and wild; then watched the silent heat lightning flash from the sultry accumulation of clouds which veiled the western sky, or solacing themselves with pipes, listened to the mournful cry of the whippoorwill and the quavering scream of the owl. Then all slept save the lone sentry, whose practical eye pierced the gloomy recesses of the forest, and whose ear caught the slightest sound, even that of the stealthy tread of the wolf and panther.

Suddenly an alarm was given that was terrible enough to quicken the pulsations of the calmest heart: A large body of savages hovered near. The garrison prepared for defense and siege; but lo! a discovery was made that intensified the alarm into terror. The supply of powder in the magazine was almost exhausted, and if an attack should be made, surrender and death at the hand of a savage foe was inevitable.

A hundred miles lay between Fort Lee and Lewisburg,—the only place from which a supply of powder could come. Col. George Clendenin summoned the garrison together and called for volunteers, for *men* who would risk their own lives, in an effort to save others. Not one would enter upon the perilous journey. Brave men looked each other in the face only to see reflected back the dismay which appalled that entire garrison. Then was heard in a determined tone the words "I WILL GO," and every inmate of that beleaguered fort recognized the voice of Anne Bailey.

The fleetest horse within the stockade was caparisoned and brought out. The commander assisted the daring rider to mount. The gate was opened and horse and rider disappeared in the forest, leaving suspense and deferred hope within the fort. Onward she sped up the Kanawha. Gauley was crossed; Kanawha's Falls left in the distance, and onward rode Anne Bailey through the voiceless forest. The Hawk's Nest appeared in sight, and from its summit her eye traced the silvery course of New River, which,

rolling like a destiny, rushed onward through
the realms of solitude and shade. Darkness and
day were one to her; she knew the route; it was
a ride for life and there could be no stop. The
shadows of night were lifted; the Greenbrier
Mountains stood out against the eastern sky; the
forests on the Lewisburg hills glistened in the
morning sunlight, and the walls of Fort Savannah
rose to view. A familiar voice; an opening of the
gates; a welcome, and Anne Bailey was telling to
the commandant the condition of affairs at Fort
Lee and the object of her mission.

The delay was short. She was furnished with
an additional horse and both were laden with
powder. The officer in command offered to send
a guard with her but this she declined and with
the two horses, the one rode, the other lead,—she
began her perilous return. Night and day she
pressed on, and at last, well nigh exhausted, but
animated by the hope of saving other's lives, she
reached Fort Lee, and amid shouts, the echoes of
which died away among the surrounding hills,
she was ushered within the gates, having accomplished the most daring feat recorded in the annals of the West. The savages still hovered
near, but the next morning, the garrison sallied

forth and after a spirited action, forced them to raise the siege and thus that feeble garrison on the site where a capital city now stands, was saved from savage butchery, and that too, by the Heroine of the Great Kanawha Valley. She was then in the forty-ninth year of her age.

The poet has sung of the deed of Elizabeth Zane who dared a storm of savage bullets at Fort Henry, but that was a life imperiled but for a moment, and who shall say that the achievement of Anne Bailey was not a far greater undertaking, for in addition to the danger of the long perilous ride, she left Fort Lee and returned to it under a savage fire.

Her deed has been commemorated in song as well as story. Charles Robb, of the United States Army was at Gauley Bridge, in 1861, and having heard the story of Anne Bailey, wrote the following, which at the time appeared in the Clermont, (Ohio) *Courier.*

ANNE BAILEY'S RIDE.

A LEGEND OF THE KANAWHA.

BY CHARLES ROBB, U. S. A.

The Army lay at Gauley Bridge,
At Mountain Cove and Sewell Ridge;
Our tents were pitched on hill and dell
From Charleston Height to Cross Lane fell;
Our camp-fires blazed on every route,
From Red House point to Camp Lookout;
On every rock our sentries stood,
Our scouts held post in every wood,
And every path was stained with blood
From Scarey creek to Gauley flood.

'Twas on a bleak autumnal day,
When not a single sunbeam's ray
Could struggle through the dripping skies
To cheer our melancholy eyes—
Whilst heavy clouds, like funeral palls,
Hung o'er Kanawha's foaming falls,
And shrouded all the mountain green
With dark, foreboding, misty screen.

All through the weary livelong day
Our troops had marched the mountain way;
And in the gloomy eventide
Had pitched their tents by the river's side;
And as the darkness settled o'er
The hill and vale and river shore,
We gathered round the camp-fire bright,
That threw its glare on the misty night;

And each some tale or legend told
To while away the rain and cold.-
Thus, one a tale of horror told
That made the very blood run cold;
One spoke of suff'ring and of wrong;
Another sang a mountain song;
One spoke of home, and happy years,
Till down his swarthy cheek the tears
Slow dripping, glistened in the light
That glared upon the misty night;
While others sat in silence deep,
Too sad for mirth, yet scorned to weep.

Then spake a hardy mountaineer—
(His beard was long, his eye was clear;
And clear his voice, of metal tone,
Just such as all would wish to own)—

"I've heard a legend old," he said,
"Of one who used these paths to tread
Long years ago, when fearful strife
Sad havoc made of human life;
A deed of daring bravely done,
A feat of honor nobly won;
And what in story 's most uncommon,
An army saved by gentle woman.

"'Twas in that dark and bloody time*
When savage craft and tory crime
From Northern lake to Southern flood,
Had drenched the western world with blood.
And in this wild, romantic glen
Encamped a host of savage men,
Whose mad'ning war-whoop, loud and high,
Was answered by the panther's cry.

*1791.

"The pale-faced settlers all had fled,
Or murdered were in lonely bed;
Whilst hut and cabin, blazing high,
With crimson decked the midnight sky.

"I said the settlers all had fled—
Their pathway down the valley led
To where the Elk's bright crystal waves
On dark Kanawha's bosom laves,
There safety sought, and respite brief,
And in Fort Charleston found relief;
Awhile they bravely met their woes,
And kept at bay their savage foes.

"Thus days and weeks the warfare waged,
In fury still the conflict raged;
Still fierce and bitter grew the strife
Where every foeman fought for life.
Thus day by day the siege went on,
Till three long, weary weeks were gone;
And then the mournful word was passed
That every day might be their last;
The word was whispered soft and slow,
The magazine was getting low.
They loaded their rifles one by one,
And then—*the powder all was gone!*
They stood like men in calm despair,
No friendly aid could reach them there;
Their doom was sealed, the scalping knife
And burning stake must end the strife.
One forlorn hope alone remained,
That distant aid might yet be gained
If trusty messenger should go
Through forest wild, and savage foe,
And safely there should bear report,
And succor bring from distant Fort.

But who should go—the venture dare?
The woodsmen quailed in mute despair,
In vain the call to volunteer;
The bravest blenched with silent fear.
Each gloomy brow and labored breath,
Proclaimed the venture worse than death.
Not long the fatal fact was kept;
But through the Fort the secret crept
Until it reached the ladies' hall,
There like a thunderbolt to fall.
Each in terror stood amazed,
And silent on the other gazed;
No word escaped—there fell no tear—
But all was hushed in mortal fear;
All hope of life at once had fled,
And filled each soul with nameless dread.
*But one** who stood amid the rest,
The bravest, fairest, and the best
Of all that graced the cabin hall,
First broke the spell of terror's thrall.
Her step was firm, her features fine,
Of Mortal mould the most divine;
But why describe her graces fair,
Her form, her mien, her stately air?
Nay, hold! my pen, I will not dare!
'Twas Heaven's image mirrored there.
She spoke no word, of fear, or boast,
But smiling, passed the sentry post;
And half in hope, and half in fear,
She whispered in her husband's ear,
The sacrifice her soul would make
Her friends to save from brand and stake.
A noble charger standing nigh,
Of spirit fine, and metal high,

*Anne Bailey.

Was saddled well, and girted strong,
With cord, and loop, and leathern thong,
For her was led in haste from stall,
Upon whose life depended all.
Her friends she gave a parting brief,
No time was there for idle grief;
Her husband's hand a moment wrung,
Then lightly to the saddle sprung;
And followed by the prayers and tears,

The kindling hopes, and boding fears
Of those who seemed the sport of fate,
She dashed beyond the op'ning gate;
Like birdling free, on pinion light,
Commenced her long and weary flight.

"The foemen saw the op'ning gate,
And thought with victory elate
To rush within the portal rude,
And in his dark and savage mood
To end the sanguinary strife
With tomahawk and scalping-knife.
But lo! a lady! fair and bright,
And seated on a charger light,
Bold—and free—as one immortal—
Bounded o'er the op'ning portal.
Each savage paused in mute surprise,
And gazed with wonder-staring eyes;
'A squaw! a squaw!' the chieftain cries,
('A squaw! a squaw!' the host replies:)
Then order gave to 'cross the lawn
With lightning speed and catch the fawn.'
Her pathway up the valley led,
Like frightened deer the charger fled,
And urged along by whip and rein,
The quick pursuit was all in vain,

A hundred bended bows were sprung,
A thousand savage echoes rung—
But far too short the arrows fell
All harmless in the mountain dell;
'To horse! to horse!' the chieftain cried,
They mount in haste and madly ride.
Along the rough, uneven way,
The pathway of the lady lay;
Whilst long and loud the savage yell
Re-echoed through the mountain fell.
She heeded not the dangers rife,
But rode as one who rides for life;
Still onward in her course she bore
Along the dark Kanawha's shore,
Through tangled wood and rocky way,
Nor paused to rest at close of day.
Like skimming cloud before the wind
Soon left the rabble far behind.
From bended tree above the road
The flying charger wildly trode,
Amid the evening's gath'ring gloom,
The panther's shriek, the voice of doom
In terror fell upon the ear,
And quickened every pulse with fear.
But e'en the subtle panther's bound,
To reach his aim too slow was found;
And headlong falling on the rock,
Lay crushed and mangled in the shock.
The prowling wolf then scents his prey,
And rushing on with angry bay,
With savage growl and quickening bound
He clears the rough and rugged ground;
And closing fast the lessening space
That all too soon must end the race,
With sharpened teeth that glittered white

As stars amid the gloomy night—
With foaming jaws had almost grasped
The lovely hand that firmly clasped,
And well had used the whip and rein,
But further effort now were vain ;
Another bound—a moment more—
And then the struggle all were o'er.
'Twas in a steep and rocky gorge
Along the river's winding verge,
Just where the foaming torrent falls
Far down through adamantine halls.
And then comes circling round and round,
As loth to leave the enchanted ground.
Just there a band of wand'ring braves
Had pitched their tents beside the waves.
The sun long since had sunk to rest,
And long the light had faded west—
When all were startled by the sound
Of howling wolf and courser's bound,
That onward came, with fearful clang,
Whose echoes round the mountain rang;
The frightened wolf in wild surprise
A moment paused—with glaring eyes
In terror gazed upon the flame,
Then backward fled the way he came.
Each wondering savage saw with fear
The charger come like frightened deer ;
With weary gait, and heavy tramp,
The foaming steed dashed through the camp
And onward up the valley bear
His queenly rider, brave and fair.
Still on, and on, through pathless wood—
They swim the Gauley's swollen flood,
And climb Mount Tompkins' lofty brow,
More wild and rugged far than now,

Still onward held their weary flight
Beyond the Hawk's Nest's Giddy Height;
And often chased through lonely glen
By savage beast or savage men—
Thus like some weary, hunted dove
The woman sped through 'Mountain Cove,'
The torrent crossed without a bridge,
And scaled the heights of Sewell Ridge,
And still the wild, beleaguered road
With heavy tramp the charger trode,
Nor paused amid his weary flight
Throughout the long and dreary night.
And bravely rode the woman there,
Where few would venture, few would dare
Amid the cheering light of day
To tread the wild beleaguered way;
And as the morning sunbeams fall
O'er hill and dale, and sylvan hall,
Far in the distance, dim and blue,
The friendly Fort* arose to view,
Whose portal soon the maiden gains
With slackened speed and loosened reins
And voice whose trembling accents tell,
Of journey ridden long and well.

"The succor thus so nobly sought,
To Charleston Fort was timely brought;
Whilst Justice, on the scroll of fame,
In letters bold, engraved her name."

GAULEY BRIDGE, VA., Nov. 7, 1861.

---

*Lewisburg.

The generation in which she lived could not repay her for the service rendered, but the garrison at Fort Lee, in appreciation thereof, promptly, on her return, voted her a present of the horse on which she had made the daring ride. He was a fine animal, black, with white feet, blazed face and glassy eyes. She named him "Liverpool," in honor of her birthplace in England, and he was thenceforth to be associated with her in many adventures.

A brief notice of the road on which the daring ride was made must prove of interest. Colonel John Stuart of Greenbrier, in a Memoir, written in 1798, thus tells of its construction:

"The paper money emitted for maintaining our war against the British became totally depreciated, and there was not a sufficient quantity of specie in circulation to enable the people to pay the revenue tax assessed upon the citizens of this county (Greenbrier), wherefore we fell in arrears to the public for four years. But the Assembly again taking our remote situation under consideration, graciously granted the sum of five thousand pounds of our said arrears to be applied to the purpose of opening a road from Lewisburg to the Kanawha river. The people, grateful for such indulgence, willingly embraced the opportunity of such an offer, and every person liable for arrears of tax agreed to perform labor equivalent on the road, and the people being formed into districts with each a superintendent, the road was completed in the space of two months in the year 1786, and thus was a communication by wagon to the navigable waters of the Kanawha first effected, and which will probably be found the nighest and best conveyance from the Eastern to the Western country that will ever be known."

It is thus seen that the road had been constructed *five* years before Anne Bailey made her historic journey over it.

The writer is unable to learn the exact date of the death of her husband, John Bailey, but it is believed to have occurred about the year 1802, at Charleston or in the vicinity. He owned a a tract of land in Kanawha county, situated on the head waters of Campbell's, Blue, Bell and Kelley's creeks, but it passed into the possession of John Barkley in 1802, and the name of John Bailey disappeared from the assessor's books after that date. He was buried on the Joseph Carroll farm, fifteen miles above Charleston, on an eminence overlooking the beautiful Kanawha, and there his remains now repose.

CHAPTER VIII.

The Treaty of Greenville in 1795, forever put an end to savage warfare in the Kanawha Valley and the influences of civilized life spread abroad over its entire extent. Among the pioneers Anne Bailey spent many years and grew old among them. Everywhere she was a most welcome guest, and she found a home wherever she stopped. A notice of those long associated with her, if but a mention of their names, must recall pleasant memories.

Colonel George Clendenin and his brothers were the founders of Charleston. Three of them, George, William and Alexander, were in the battle of Point Pleasant, the first being then but seventeen years of age. His wife was Geneive McNeale, a sister of the wife of General Thomas Ewing, of Ohio.

He had issue a daughter, Parthena, who married first R. J. Meigs, of Marietta, Ohio. They removed to Paris, Kentucky, where the husband died leaving the widow with one son, R. J. Meigs, who at the age of ninety years, now lives in Washington City. The widow returned to Point Pleasant, where, June 1st, 1809, she wedded Andrew Bryan, by whom she had issue four children, the eldest being Mary—now the aged Mrs. Mary McCulloch, of Mason county, who is the nearest living relative of the founder of Charleston. She has an excellent memory, unimpaired by age, and she well remembers Anne Bailey, she often being a guest at the Bryan home.

William Clendenin, brother of George, left Fort Lee at Charleston, in 1797, and settled on the Ohio, nine miles above Point Pleasant, but in 1802, he removed four miles below the mouth of the Kanawha, where he reared his cabin and cleared the first acre of land improved on Mercer's Bottom. Here Anne Bailey, in her later years, often delighted the neighbors with the recital of her adventures.

The garrison at old Fort Randolph had left its walls and were living around Point Pleasant. Among them were John Van Bibber,

Mathias Van Bibber, John Reynolds, Isaac Tyler, Michael See, Benjamin Eulin and Luman Gibbs. The latter was a famous scout. Born in New Hampshire in 1755, he came to Virginia just in time to enlist in the army of General Lewis, and later, participated in the battle of Point Pleasant. He was one of the men detailed to build the fort after the battle. Here he soon became a famous scout, and for twenty long, dark and bloody years, he served in that capacity, wandering over the neighboring hills with his rifle in his hand and the love of his fellowmen in his heart; and rarely was it that the savages reached the Valley, that their movements were not watched by his unwearied eye. Weekly he sallied forth from the fort and proceeded up the Kanawha to the mouth of Eighteen Mile creek; thence through the wilderness to Letart Falls, and thence down the Ohio, to Point Pleasant, where his report of "All is well," dispelled for the time the fear of massacre from those confined within the fort. So well was his route known, that by the early settlers, it was called "Gibb's Trace." He died in 1839, and is buried about eight miles from Point Pleasant. By his side sleep James Ball and Isaac Robinson, soldiers in the battle of Point Pleasant and heroes of the Revolution.

Prominent among those with whom Anne Bailey lived, was Captain William Arbuckle. He was born of Scotch-Irish parentage, near Balcony Falls on James river in the year 1746. His entire life and best energies were contributed to wrest this fair domain from the sway of savage men, and his entire life was characterized by noble acts performed in this effort to settle the wilderness. In every walk of life, he was as truly great as Daniel Boone, or Simon Kenton. When General Lewis was collecting his army at Camp Union, preparatory to the campaign of 1774, William Arbuckle was among the first to enroll his name in Captain Stewart's company, in which he served to the close of Dunmore's War, having distinguished himself on the bloody field at Point Pleasant, and also by his determined opposition to Dunmore after the army reached the Pickaway Plains. He witnessed the murder of Cornstalk at Point Pleasant, November 10, 1777, and risked his life to prevent it. In 1778, he joined the expedition of Colonel Clarke against the British posts in Illinois and Indiana, the most remarkable military movement recorded in the history of

the West. Three hundred men entered upon the
march of 600 miles through a trackless wilderness and after many days toiling through almost
impassable swamps, the waters of which were in
many places waist deep, they reached their desti-
nation and by stratagem, succeeded in surprising
and capturing three of the strongest fortifications
in the West. Returning to the Valley, we find
him by the side of his brother Mathew, Captain
John Stuart, Jesse Van Bibber and others defending the settlements against the incursions of
the Indians. Soon after he came to the Kanawha, he wedded Catharine, the beautiful and accomplished widow of Captain Robert McClena-
han, who fell at Point Pleasant. She was a cou-
sin of James Madison, fourth president of the
United States. After their marriage, they settled at Fort Savannah—now Lewisburg—in which
Jane, who subsequently became the wife of Joseph McMullin, was born. Removing to Point
Pleasant, he had two daughters born in Fort
Randolph. When the war was over he settled
on the Kanawha, four miles below where Buffalo
now stands, where both he and his wife lived to
a ripe old age, and when they had seen their
children well settled in life, and the wilderness

blossom as the rose, and had seen the transit of
palatial steamers on the Kanawha, and when
churches and school houses had been reared about
them, then they died and found a grave near by
where they had found a home. Anne Bailey was
ever a welcome guest in their hospitable home.

Daniel Boone was also a resident of the Valley.
The cause which led to his removal from Kentucky, is but another instance of man's injustice
to man. Boone had been the first white man to
find a home in the wilds of Kentucky; he had discovered its wonderful resources and had proclaimed them to the world. His footsteps had been marked in blood. Two darling sons had fallen by savage
hands amid the gloomy defiles of the Allegheny
mountains. Many dark and sleepless nights he
had been the companion of wild beasts, separated
from the society of civilized men, scorched by the
summer's sun and chilled by the winter's blast—
he was an instrument ordained to settle the wilderness. When the storm of war had died away
and Boone had settled upon his lands, the sheriff
suddenly entered the cabin and informed him that
the title to his lands was disputed, and that legal
proceedings had been instituted against him.
Boone could not understand this. Kentucky, he

regarded as his own by the right of discovery. He had led the way there; he had established himself and family in the land and now in his advancing years, to be driven from that home seemed unjust indeed. He made no defense and, stung by ingratitude, he turned his eyes to the distant home of his childhood on the Schuylkill, from which he had wandered forty years before. But there, all was changed and amid blooming orchards and cultivated fields, there could be no home for him. Forever leaving the scene, he came to the Kanawha Valley, where he found congenial spirits with whom he spent ten or twelve years of his life. With George Clendenin, he represented Kanawha County in the General Assembly of Virginia, in 1791, and about the year 1798, sought and found a home with his son, Daniel M. Boone, in the wilds of Upper Louisana. There he died in 1820, and in 1845, his remains were removed to Frankfort, Kentucky, where they now repose.

Then there was Captain Jesse VanBibber, who when the wars were past, built his cabin on Thirteen Mile Creek ,now in Mason County. He was the first settler on that stream. His early life, like the mountain stream on which he settled, was rough in the extreme. Born on the frontier, he early in life became inured to hardships and privations experienced only by pioneers of the wilderness. The bloody scenes in which the tomahawk and scalping knife played prominent parts were those with which he had grown familiar, having witnessed the murder and scalping of his own niece Rhoda VanBibber on the banks of the Ohio opposite Point Pleasant. He was a soldier during Dunmore's War, serving in the southern wing of the army, when he was eulogized by General Lewis for his bravery displayed on the field at Point Pleasant. From 1774 to 1795, he was constantly engaged in the military affairs of the Valley. His commission as captain is in the archives of the West Virginia Historical and Antiquarian Society. During Boone's sojourn in the Valley, he was often the guest of Captain VanBibber and many times they were companions in the chase. It was on the occasion of one of their hunts on the waters of Thirteen, that Boone bestowed the name of "Mud Lick" upon the principal tributary of that stream. Far up it, is a lick or salt spring, which at that time, was kept muddy constantly by the animals that resorted thither in quest of the brackish waters.

Here in the depth of the forest these two pilots
of the wilderness spent many a night awaiting
the approach of the game which, rarely if ever,
failed to become the victims of their deadly rifles. When speaking of this locality, Boone re-
ferred to it as the Mud Lick creek and long years
after Captain Van Bibber informed the settlers,
as they came in, that Boone had named the
stream. They were willing that it should retain
the name bestowed upon it by the founder of
Kentucky, and by that name it is known to-day.
Captain Van Bibber, late in life, became a member of the Baptist church, and as his eventful
life drew to a close, it beautifully reflected the
Christian character. He died in 1847, and is
buried near where he spent the last years of his
life. His home was one of Anne Bailey's favorite stopping places, and here with the old soldier,
was rehearsed the past story of their eventful
lives.

Of all the warriors who established homes in
the Valley of the Kanawha, none were braver or
more honored than the Coopers. Major Leonard
Cooper held a commission in the military establishment of Maryland, and when he learned of
the westward march of General Lewis, he hast-

ened to Staunton and tendered his services, which were accepted and he participated in the battle of Point Pleasant. Returning east he served in a Maryland regiment to the close of the Revolutionary war. In 1785, in company with Thomas Teays and John Turley, he visited Point Pleasant and on their return up the Valley, they encamped for the night at the mouth of Scarey creek. In the night their horses strayed away and Cooper and Teays, the next morning went in search of them. When just below the creek, they were fired upon by a party of eight Indians and Teays was killed. Cooper, unhurt, jumped from his horse, crossed the creek and escaped up the mountain. He supposed that Turley was killed at camp for the reason that he heard firing in that direction. This was doubtless true for Turley was never afterward heard of. In 1789, Major Cooper removed with his family to Point Pleasant and in 1794 erected what was for many years known as Cooper's Blockhouse. It stood on the north bank of the Kanawha, about nine miles from Point Pleasant and on lands now owned by George W. Pullins, Esq. Here Major Cooper continued to reside until the time of his death, in 1808. When Mason county was formed in 1804, Major Cooper became one of the justices of the new county and as such continued until his death. During his residence at the mouth of the Kanawha, his son Leonard was born. The year was 1791, and he was the first white child born at Point Pleasant. How strong the ties were that bound Anne Bailey to the Cooper family the sequel will show.

Far down on Mercer's bottom lived Captain John Hereford. He was one of the earliest settlers in what is now Mason county, coming from Fairfax county, Virginia, in 1790. He was an ardent patriot during the Revolution and for his gallantry on the field of battle was promoted to the rank of adjutant, serving under Colonels John Alexander and George West, each commanding Virginia regiments, and with the latter he was at the siege of Yorktown. Few men have enjoyed a higher reputation for sterling integrity. In his nature, brave, generous and magnanimous, he commanded the respect and esteem of those around him. He died May 13, 1846, in the eighty-ninth year of his age. He had been a soldier and certainly Anne Baily would find a welcome in his home.

There, too, resided Joseph H. Holloway on the

farm now owned by John W. Steenbergen. He was from that part of Botetourt, now included in Allegheny, where he wedded Mary Hinton. He was a soldier in the war of 1812. He and his wife had known Anne Bailey long before they came to Mercer's Bottom, and with them she spent much of her time, especially in the later years of her life.

Our heroine was often a visitor at the residence of Dr. Jesse Bennett, six miles up the Ohio from Point Pleasant. He was born in 1749, in Pennsylvania, near the spot that gave birth to Daniel Boone. Graduating in medicine in Philadelphia, he wedded Elizabeth, the daughter of Peter Hogg, the king's Prosecutor of Dunmore, (now Shenandoah) county, in the colony of Virginia, and in 1797, in company with his brother-in-law, William Hawkins, settled at Six Mile Island, now in Mason county, which he represented in the General Assembly of Virginia, in 1808. In 1812, he went, as surgeon, with the Mason county Riflemen to the Maumee. He died in 1842, having been the first regularly educated physician that practiced his profession in the Valley of the Kanawha.

We have not space to notice in detail all of the

early settlers with whom Anne Baily was familiar
and at whose hospitable houses she was so often
a welcome guest. Among them in addition
to those mentioned on Mercer's Bottom were:
Thomas Hannan, Thomas Powell, Edward S.
Menager, John Morris, George Withers, James
George, Andrew Wallace, William P. Hereford,
Esom Hannan, Bailey Holley and Reuben Cre-
means. Near where Leon now stands lived Jacob
Mackley, Theophilus McCoy, Robert Pruit,
Michael See, James Kingsbury, Maurice Green-
lee, Samuel Smith, Boudridge Warner, Joseph
Harrison and James Nelson. Near the present
site of Buffalo were Jonathan Hill, Ira Dilno
and Thomas Scott, while at Charleston and in the
vicinity, were Joseph, David and Tobias Ruffner,
Fleming Cobb, Mathias Van Bibber, Jacob Young,
Lewis Tackett, Andrew Donnally, William,
Henry and Leonard Morris, John Reynolds, John
Hansford, Paddy Huddlestons, Shadrach Harri-
man, Robert McKee, John Wilson and many
others. The latter married Catharine, the daughter of Andrew Donnally, the builder and defender
of Fort Donnally in Greenbrier, and settled near
Springhill, in Kanawha county. He was Captain
of the Kanawha Volunteers in the war of 1812.

His house was a favorite stopping place for Anne Bailey and there she ever found a hearty welcome.

Beyond the Ohio, four miles below Point Pleasant, at what is now Gallipolis, the representatives of another nation had escaped the horrors of the French Revolution and had found a home on the banks of the Ohio. Joel Barlow in 1790, as the agent of the Scioto Land Company had appeared in Paris and, in the street Rue Neuve, des Petits Champs, had offered for sale at a French crown per acre, three million acres of land situated on the Ohio river in what was then the Northwest Territory. Sales were rapidly made, and in 1791 ships left the port of Havre de Grace, having on board large numbers of emigrants bound for the new Canaan on the banks of the Ohio. In time they were landed at Alexandria, Virginia, whence they wended their way over the mountains by way of Winchester, Brownsville, and thence down *la Belle Riviere* and in the months of October, November and December, between four and five hundred French emigrants landed at Gallipolis. All was gaiety and music of a high order, for the first time vibrated through the solitudes of the wilderness. The founders of Gallipolis—the City of the Gauls—were then upon the scene where they laid the foundations of that culture and refinement which has characterized their descendants in later days.

Soon Anne Bailey was a visitor within the cabins which then adorned what is now the city park. These Frenchmen, and their sons, wives and daughters heard the story of her life. With them she found a hearty welcome, and thenceforth she was, to the end of her life, a familiar figure on the streets and in the homes of that town.

CHAPTER IX.

REMINISCENCES OF ANNE BAILEY—HER TWENTY-
SEVEN YEAR'S RESIDENCE IN THE
KANAWHA VALLEY.

After her famous ride from Fort Lee to Lewisburg, Anne Bailey appears to have abandoned all
thought of a fixed habitation, and thenceforth,
mounted on her favorite horse, "Liverpool," she
ranged all the country from Point Pleasant to
Staunton.

Surrounded with peace and quiet, her heroism
might have slumbered, but contact with the wilderness was a rude touchstone, which developed
traits that would have remained dormant, and
therefore would have remained unsuspected in
civilized life.

She was a tower of adamant against which hard-
ship, danger, the rage of the savages and of the
elements, fatigue and hunger emptied their qui-

vers in vain. Never under the impenetrable coat of
mail of crusader, beat a heart actuated by greater
heroism and ardent love for humanity, than that
which throbbed within the breast of Anne Bailey.

She was a stranger to fear, and while men were
still subjected to garrison duty in the border
stockade forts, she boldly sallied forth into the
wilderness as if to challenge the ferocity of wild
beasts and the vengeance of savage men. Day
and night she continued on the journey, and
many times slept in the wilderness with only her
faithful horse tied near by.

The rigors of winter had no terrors for her.
On one occasion when on a journey from Charleston to Lewisburg, darkness overtook her when
amid the storm-swept Alleghenies. It was bitter
cold, and to prevent freezing, she sought and
found a hollow tree into which she crept and then
held her horse so that he constantly blew his
breath upon her, and was thus saved from freezing.

Dr. D. C. Forbes, for a number of years a
practitioner at Leon, on the Kanawha, informed
the writer several years since, that when he first
came to the Valley, there was a cave under a

shelving rock on the hillside just below the mouth of Thirteen Mile Creek, that was locally known as "Anne Bailey's Cave," and that he was informed by the old settlers, several of whom were then living, that here she spent many a night. Leaving the fort at Charleston, she would ride this far, find shelter for the night and then proceed to Point Pleasant the next morning. The doctor expressed regret that in his temporary absence, workmen quarried the rock and thus obliterated one of the historic land-marks of the Valley.

It is related that once when on a journey from Point Pleasant to Charleston and when a short distance above where Winfield is now situated, she was discovered by a wandering band of savages. They gave chase, and she, finding that she would be overtaken, dismounted from her horse and, escaping unto the underbrush, concealed herself in the hollow of a sycamore log. The Indians made extended search for her and halted to rest on the log in which she was concealed, but at length departed taking her horse with them. Late in the evening she crept forth from her hiding-place and taking the trail of the Indians, followed it until she came in view of their encampment. Then

awaiting the cover of darkness, and while they
slept, she quietly stole up and untieing Liverpool,
sprang upon his back and when a short distance
away, she uttered a scream of defiance and riding
rapidly, reached Charleston in safety. So often did
she thus baffle the Indians, that they came to believe that she was a charmed being. The Shaw-
nee warriors knew her as "The white Squaw of
the Kanawha." First, because of her reckless
daring, they believed her to be insane, and they
ever regarded one in that condition as being under the special care of the Great Spirit. Then,
in their superstition, they beheld her as the "phantom rider," which appeared here, there and everywhere on their paths. They saw her glide through
the dark foliage on the plains of the Kanawha,
and from the mountain summits they beheld her
as she galloped along the rocky and narrow defiles of the Alleghenies. To the Indian, everything that he did not comprehend, was attributed
to a supernatural agency, and then he held it in the
greatest awe and reverence. To this fact, Anne
Bailey probably owed her life, for these forest
warriors were so much impressed with what
seemed to them to be an apparition or phantom
that they feared even from ambush to send the

arrow or bullet after her. Thus rode the "White Squaw of the Kanawha," of whom the Indians themselves long retained a tradition.

At last the savage no more visited the Valley of the Kanawha, and when the pioneers practiced war no more, they engaged in the peaceful avocations of civilized life, but for Anne Bailey, there could be no permanent home. The only home that she could know, was that of others. The military spirit was so fully developed in her, that to the day of her death, she continued that adventurous career the long period of border life had made second nature to her, and for years, mounted on horseback, she was a conspicuous figure in all the country from Gallipolis and Point Pleasant to Staunton.

At the former places and along the Kanawha, were many families, who were hundreds of miles from the necessaries of life, not to mention the conveniences. There were no postoffices; not a pound of coffee, powder or lead within a hundred miles; and these, if obtained at all, must be brought from Lewisburg or Staunton.

Here, then, was a field and an occupation for Anne Bailey, and well did she improve it. From the French at Gallipolis, where she had become a

great favorite; from the dwellers at Point Pleasant
and along the Kanawha, she obtained orders for the
articles most in need, and then rode away to Lewisburg, where she secured them if they were there
to be had, but if not, then the journey was extended
to Staunton, from which, with her horse frequently
so heavily laden, that she walked and lead him,
and thus was brought to the Valley, coffee for
one, drugs for another, powder for another, a
farming utensil for another and so on through the
list of absolute necessities. She frequently purchased articles when at Staunton, of which she
made sale in the Kanawha Valley. The venerable James H. Holloway, of Point Pleasant, re-
cently informed the writer that he, when a boy,
purchased from her, the first pocket-knife he ever
owned.

The writer, a few weeks since, asked the aged
Mrs. Mary McCulloch, of Mason county, who
well remembers Anne Bailey, about the business
in which she was engaged, and in reply, she
said: "Oh, yes; she would bring anything that
a horse could carry, just like an express company, and she was honest to a cent. Money was
scarce, and the people could not make change,
but no matter what amount they gave

Anne Bailey, every cent of it was accounted
for."

Think of it! Anne Bailey doing a regular
express business, in the Kanawha Valley nearly
a hundred years ago. She antedated Alvin Ad-
ams, Ephraim Farnesworth and William Harn-
den, by nearly half a century, and who shall say
that if she would have had energetic successors
who would have continued the business thus began by her, the Bailey Express Company would
not to-day be one of the greatest public carriers
in all the land?

If it was hogs or cattle that was wanted she
drove them through, if she had to go to the banks
of the Shenandoah for them. There is a tradition, current for nearly a hundred years, that she
brought the first tame geese to the Kanawha
Valley. Captain William Clendenin, soon after
his removal to Mercer's Bottom, entered into a
contract with her to bring him a number of tame
geese from the Greenbrier Valley, where they
had been introduced previously from the Shenandoah Valley. The contract was in keeping
with the Captain's exact methods of transacting
business, and specified that the number should
be just *twenty,* else he would not pay for them.

Anne Bailey went to Greenbrier, where she collected the required number and drove them through to the Kanawha. When near Charleston one of the number died, and, remembering the terms of the contract, she dismounted and putting the dead goose in a bag, proceeded on to Clendenin's where, upon her arrival, she drove the flock into the yard. The Captain carefully counted the number and finding that there were but *nineteen,* said: "Well, Anne, you did not bring the number named in the contract and I can not pay for them." She, with a business mein equal to that of the Captain, walked out to where she had hitched her horse, and, taking the *dead* goose from the bag, threw it down in the yard, and remarked, "There's your twenty." The Captain saw where the contract was defective, and promptly paid the bill.

Biography should be a true portraiture of the subject, else it fails of its chief uses in literature, for it is worthless save for the examples it presents. What of the character of Anne Bailey? It has been asserted that she indulged in profanity and drank to intoxication. In an effort to ascertain the truthfulness of this statement the writer has in the past fifteen years, made careful

inquiry of more than a dozen persons, all of
whom knew her and some of whom are yet living,
relative to the moral character of Anne Bailey,
and here gives the results:

Mrs. Rebecca Clendenin, formerly of Mason
county, now deceased, stated that when a small
girl, she once went to the house of Captain Clendenin and found him and Anne Bailey engaged
in an animated discussion, relative to some past
event, while a bottle of brandy sat on the table
near by. They could not agree and it was de-
cided that they should compromise the matter by
taking a drink, which they did. Beyond this,
no evidence of intoxication has been found. She
would take a drink but we must remember that
in a new country, a hundred years ago, that was
not looked upon as it is to-day by a more polite
society. There is no evidence that she ever indulged in profanity.

The aged Mrs. Mary Irions, of Gallia county,
Ohio, and a grand-daughter of the subject, said
to the writer: "Grandma did not belong to any
church but she was a good woman. She never
used bad language; she carefully observed the
Sabbath and many times I have heard her pray."

What more was needed? Heroism, virtue, integrity, mercy, benevolence, observance of the Sabbath and a dependence upon that Providence which had protected her all along an eventful pathway of life, all blended, make up the character of Anne Bailey, the Pioneer Heroine of the Kanawha Valley.

She could not bear the thought of annihilation —of ceasing to exist, and it is related that she frequently gave expression to the thought that in the hereafter, she would rather exist in misery than not to exist at all.

CHAPTER X.

Years came and went and Anne Bailey grew
old. Long she had gone on foot from one extreme of the Valley to the other, stopping where
she pleased and staying as long as she pleased,
for she was welcome everywhere. From what
can be now learned, it is believed that she
made her last visit to Charleston in the summer
of 1817.

The late venerable Laban Hill, of Mason
county, who when a mere youth, accompanied
his father, Jonathan Hill, to a pioneer home on
Eighteen Mile creek, now in Putnam county, in
1816, informed the writer some years ago, that in
the spring of 1817, he went to spend the night at
the house of Ira Dilno, a neighbor of his father,
and that late in the evening, there arrived no less
a distinguished personage than Anne Bailey, then

in the 75th year of her age and *walking* to
Charleston to visit friends. This statement is
verified by that of Robert Warth, Esq., aged
ninety-two years, of Ravenswood, West Virginia,
who is still living and who says that he met her
about six miles above Charleston, walking toward
that place, in the summer of 1817.

No evidence of a later visit appears and it is
presumed that in that year, she for the last time
visited the associates of more eventful years.
How long she remained we do not know, but Mr.
Hill says he saw her in the *spring*. Mr. Warth
says it was in the summer when he saw her near
Charleston. She therefore probably spent several
weeks or possibly months on and near the scenes
of many of her adventures.

It is seventy-four years since Anne Bailey was
on the streets of Charleston. What changes
have taken place since that time! Then, clad in her
border costume, she went from house to house
and in all, the story of that perilous ride, and a
hundred other adventures, was recited. A new
generation had appeared and the rehearsals found
listening ears. Imagine Anne Bailey passing
along Capitol street to-day. What a remarkable
personage she would be! How strange would be

the contrast where now move a cultured and re-
fined people, enjoying every luxury which wealth
can buy. But they would do honor to the memory of Anne Bailey.

It will be remembered that when Anne Bailey
entered upon her career of adventure and daring,
she left her fatherless son, William, then but
seven years of age, under the protection of Mrs.
Moses Mann, then of Augusta, but later, of Bath
county.

How long he remained at the Mann homestead,
we have no means of knowing. Whether he
grew to manhood in Augusta, or came with his
mother and step-father to the Kanawha Valley,
cannot now be learned, but certain it is that soon
after the erection of Cooper's blockhouse, on the
Kanawha, he was there a frequent visitor. There
he woed and won the heart and hand of Mary
Ann Cooper, who was the daughter of Leonard
Cooper, who was as brave a man as ever found a
home on the banks of the Kanawha. In the year
1800, William Trotter, then in the thirty-third
year of his age, took his affianced, in a canoe to
Gallipolis, where they became husband and wife
and a tradition states that they were the first Virginians married in the old French town.

William Trotter appears to have been a practical business man at the time of his marriage, was possessed of some means. In 1814, he purchased for the sum of twelve hundred and seventy-five dollars, a tract of two hundred and forty-six acres of land situated on the south side of the Kanawha, about three miles from its mouth. This land was part of Washington's survey of ten thousand nine hundred acres, which he surveyed for himself in October, 1770. Fielding Lewis, of Hanover county, Virginia, as one of the Washington heirs, inherited thirteen hundred acres of this land, two hundred and forty-six acres of which passed into the possession of his son, Robert Lewis, the entire estate being divided among the heirs of Fielding Lewis, by survey made by Robert McKee, surveyor of Mason county, August 30th, 1813. The portion of the land inherited by Robert Lewis was sold by Henry C. Dade, his attorney in fact, to William Trotter.

Here he built a house and continued to reside three years, his heroic mother making her home with him, when he sold the land to William Sterrett, the consideration being fourteen hundred dollars, current money of Virginia. The deed of transfer bearing date March 18, 1817, may be seen in Deed Book D., page 229, in the Mason county Clerk's office.

Now, without a permanent home, he looked around and not finding a satisfactory purchase, he passed beyond the Ohio and in the year, 1818, in what is now Harrison Township, Gallia county, Ohio, bought two tracts of land, one of one hundred acres, from Paul Fearing, and another of two hundred and sixty acres, from Benjamin Joy. There he removed with his family the same year.

CHAPTER XI.

Anne Bailey was bitterly opposed to the removal North of the Ohio. Fifty-seven years she had spent in Virginia. Here were her friends and companions in war and in peace. Here slept all that was mortal of both her husbands, and now, at the age of seventy-six years, it seemed hard indeed, that she must be severed from the scenes of so many years to find a home among strangers. But the best interests of an only son were there, and with him she must go.

The home was selected in what was then the wilderness, back from the Ohio, about six miles from what is now Clipper Mills post-office, Gallia county, Ohio. Here the son plead with the mother to stay with him, but she refused to do so. If she must be severed from her Virginia friends, she had others at Gallipolis, and she would be near them.

She returned there, and on the hill just below the town and overlooking the Ohio, she reared with her own hands a pen of fence-rails which she covered and thatched with straw, and in it attempted to live. An excellent view of it together with the portrait of Anne Bailey, is shown in the frontispiece, which the author has permission to use, through the kindness of Henry Howe, Esq., the venerable historian and the distinguished author of the "Historical Collections of Ohio."

Here she remained but a short time, for her son came and with the aid of friends induced her to accompany him to his home. There she consented to remain upon the condition that he would build, near by his own, a cabin in which she should dwell alone. This he did and there she spent the remainder of her life.

For years she was a familiar character on the streets of Gallipolis where she was often a visitor. Usually she walked the entire distance of nine miles, but frequently she came up in a canoe which she could manage with the dexterity of an Indian.

On the streets she carried her rifle, and when interrogated as to the accuracy with which she could use it, would relate, in the broadest English accent, how she once sat upon the back of her favorite horse "Liverpool" and shot "a howl on a helm tree across the mouth of Helk river." With increasing age came many eccentricities, and she became known as "Mad Anne;" but none ever dared to so designate her in her presence, and as long as she was able to visit Gallipolis, she found a welcome in the hospitable homes of the French settlers at that place. Then her canoe often lay at rest beneath the willows on the Virginia shore, while she visited friends of the olden time on Mercer's Bottom.

But an eventful life was now near its close. Early Tuesday morning, November 22nd, 1825, she came from her own cabin to that of her son's, and informed her daughter-in-law that she was going to Gallipolis that day, and at the time complained of being ill. The daughter-in-law insisted that she should lie down, have some breakfast and go to town on the morrow, when she would feel better. She yielded and remained in bed until late in the evening, when she arose and persisted against persuasion in going to her own cabin, but asked that two of her grand-children—Phebe, aged eight, and Jane Anne, aged six, should accompany her. Certainly they were anxious to go with grandma, and after penning the ducks for the night, and filled with glee at the thought of staying all night with grandma, ran along the path ahead of her and the trio reached the humble cabin. A fire was built and they—youth and old age—sat around it, the little ones listening in delight to the many stories related by grandma, who loved to entertain the eager ears.

The shades of night gathered, and darkness settled around that lonely cabin. There was but one bed; the cold, chilling winds of November blew fiercely outside, and the bed was taken from the stead, spread down before the fire and the three—the little one in the middle—nestled down for the night. The fire smouldered on the hearth and the light faded into darkness. All slept, but Phebe grew cold, and but half awake, called aloud to her grand-mother, but no answer came. In her fright she called again, but all was still; then in her terror she awoke the little one and told her that grandma was dead. Without clothing and beneath the starlight, the little naked

limbs, exposed to the wintry blast, and bare feet in
the sparkling frost, they ran screaming toward
home. Fond parents heard the wails of the little
ones and hastened to meet them. They told the
story of death, and Mr. Trotter, with some men who
had been assisting him in gathering corn, hastened
away and entering the cabin, found that the soul
had passed from earth and the great heart that
had throbbed with patriotism and love for eighty-
three years, was stilled forever. Anne Bailey,
the Heroine of the Great Kanawha Valley, had
passed to eternal rest.*

Then there was a gathering of the settlers from
all around, who came to perform the last sad rites
of humanity. George Waugh who lived hard
by, made a rustic coffin, and without a funeral
service, for no minister was near, all that was
mortal of her who saved the garrison at Fort Lee,
was laid to rest in what is still known as the
Trotter Graveyard and in an unmarked and almost nameless grave, sleeps all that was earthly
of Anne Bailey. England gave her birth; Virginia, a field for action; Ohio has her dust.

The birth or death of the great has given ce-

---

*The facts here given relative to the death and burial were obtained from the
aged Mrs. Phebe Willey, of Clipper Mills, Ohio, who was the elder of the grand-
children sleeping with Anne Bailey the night of her death.

lebrity to spots of earth, and that in which Anne
Bailey sleeps should not be forgotten. As long
as heroism is appreciated by a free people, that
long should the memory of those who have given
the best examples of it, be cherished, and the
grave of Anne Bailey should be marked by a
shaft of enduring marble. But give the school
children of Gallia county, and the Kanawha Valley an opportunity, and they will erect it.

ANNE BAILEY'S DESCENDANTS.

William Trotter, as has been stated, removed
to Gallia county, Ohio, March 22, 1818. There
he became a large land owner, and was for many
years one of the Justices of the Peace for that
county. He died March 26, 1831, aged sixty-
four years, and is buried on an eminence overlooking the Ohio, three-fourths of a mile below
Clipper Mills. His wife survived him more than
forty years and is buried by his side.

They had issue:

1. Philip, born in 1801; married Hannah Cod-
   dington, of Lawrence county, Ohio, and became the father of three daughters and one son.
2. Elizabeth, born in 1803; married William C.
   Irion, and had issue, four sons and three
   daughters, one of the former dying in infancy.

3. John, born in 1805; in 1832 he rode to Gallipolis, left his horse hitched to a post and was
   never afterward heard of.
4. William, born in 1807; wedded Rosanna
   Houck, of Gallia county, and yet survives.
   They had issue, five daughters and three sons.
5. Mary, born February 11, 1811; wedded James
   Irion, and yet lives. She is the mother of
   six sons and six daughters.
6. Davis, born in 1813; wedded Sarah Knight,
   and had two sons. He died at Rockport, Indiana, several years ago.
7. Sarah, born in 1816; married John Gilmore,
   of Gallia county, and became the mother of
   five sons and two daughters.
8. Phebe, born January 6, 1818; married Thomas
   Willey, in 1851, and had issue, four daughters,
   the youngest of whom married John Williams,
   present post-master atClipper Mills. Phebe was
   the elder of the grand-children who were sleeping with Anne Bailey the night of her death.
9. Jane Anne, born in 1820; married John S.
   Northup, of Gallia county, and became the
   mother of two sons and one daughter. She
   was the little one who slept in the middle on
   that night of death.

10. Nancy, born in 1822; wedded Francis Strait, of Gallia county, and had issue, six sons.

Thus it is seen that of Anne Bailey, there is a long line of descendants, now scattered over the West and South and numbering from two to three hundred. Wherever they have gone they give evidence of having inherited that endurance, physical strength and longevity, which distinguished her from whom they are descended. Brooks Irion, one of her great-grand-sons, in 1881, at Poughkeepsie, New York, ran five hundred miles against time, winning by two hours and eight minutes. The following year he went to Europe, and in Edinburgh, Scotland, ran a hundred mile race in which he broke the world's record by five hours and thirty-five minutes and was thus regarded as the swiftest man on foot then living. Returning home he engaged in the study of law and is now practicing in Kansas.

Of all her descendants but one, Simeon Irion, Esq., of Charleston, is now living in the Kanawha Valley.

FINIS.